A CAREER IN
MINING
AND
LOGGING

Jobs for
REBUILDING AMERICA™

A CAREER IN
MINING
AND
LOGGING

Rosen
YA™

New York

JEANNE NAGLE

Published in 2019 by The Rosen Publishing Group, Inc.
29 East 21st Street, New York, NY 10010

First Edition

Library of Congress Cataloging-in-Publication Data

Names: Nagle, Jeanne, author.
Title: A career in mining and logging / Jeanne Nagle.
Description: New York : Rosen Publishing, 2019. | Series: Jobs for rebuilding America | Includes bibliographical references and index. | Audience: Grades 7–12.
Identifiers: LCCN 2017058539| ISBN 9781508179993 (library bound) | ISBN 9781508180005 (pbk.)
Subjects: LCSH: Mining engineering—Vocational guidance—Juvenile literature. | Logging—Vocational guidance—Juvenile literature.
Classification: LCC TN160 .N34 2019 | DDC 622.023—dc23
LC record available at https://lccn.loc.gov/2017058539

Manufactured in the United States of America

CONTENTS

Simply put, countries, states, and cities would not exist without solid infrastructure. These places, and the governmental leadership that oversees them, depend upon certain services in order to function as they should. Among these services, which together make up infrastructure, are transportation, communication, energy, roads, and building.

In order for infrastructure to run smoothly and efficiently, communities turn to private industry and the public sector to supply the manpower and materials that make such services possible. In other words, many different businesses employ workers with the skill sets and expertise that make a location's infrastructure tick. A number of career fields fall into this category, including mining and logging.

Mining involves digging beneath Earth's crust in order to get to deposits of valuable minerals. These materials

These coal miners certainly know the real meaning of the saying, "It's a dirty job, but somebody's got to do it." Mining, logging, and other jobs in resource extraction often mean long hours and tough working conditions.

are extracted from soil, rock, and sand and processed in a way that makes them ready for infrastructure uses such as building and energy. Logging works in much the same way, with the same goals in mind, only the resources loggers concentrate on—trees—are found above ground.

Each field is based on manual labor, which is a fancy way to say the work can get quite physical. In the past, most mining and logging tasks were performed by hand, making physical fitness a priority for people employed in these fields. Even with an increased use of computerization, which is finding its way into more jobs within these industries, mining and logging still require a great deal of physical strength and stamina. Some loggers still climb trees as part of their job, and heavy lifting is still required in many cases.

Miners may now use huge extracting machines instead of digging by hand with a pickaxe, but shoveling, lifting, and pulling still factor into their job requirements.

Working as a miner or logger is not without its drawbacks. Given work conditions and environments, there is also a certain amount of risk involved in these fields. Mining and logging regularly rank as two of the most dangerous jobs a person can undertake. The chance of onsite accidents causing serious injury, as well as health threats from being exposed to the elements or breathing toxic air underground, has turned some people away from mining and logging. Using machines to complete some of the more dangerous tasks, and instituting and adhering to strict safety regulations, help counterbalance the negatives.

There are several benefits that make these fields appealing. Some people appreciate that several jobs within these fields can be won without a college degree. Although employers might require a degree or certificate from a technical school for some positions, mining and logging also make good use of on-the-job training, particularly at the entry level.

Mining and logging also are not typical nine-to-five office careers. People in these professions operate out in nature, whether underground, on steep mountain slopes, or in an earthen pit or dense forests. Even on the processing end, workers labor in factories, not tall skyscrapers or office complexes—each of which, coincidentally, both mining and logging would have had a hand in building as part of a town's or city's infrastructure.

CHAPTER ONE

THE MINING INDUSTRY

Mining has a long and storied history in the United States. Virginia was originally colonized in the hopes that certain materials, including precious metals, could be sent back to bolster the British economy. (In the seventeenth century, the Jamestown colonists managed to extract enough iron ore from area bogs, but that was about it.) By the early eighteenth century, copper mines had been opened in Connecticut and New Jersey, while coal production began in Virginia, Pennsylvania, and Rhode Island by the late 1700s. Gold and silver mines out west, in California and Nevada, respectively, created get-rich booms in the 1800s. Yet it was coal and iron mining in other states during the same period that truly boosted the nation's economy.

The nineteenth century ushered in an era of industrialization to the United States, during which time mined materials, particularly iron ore and coal, helped the United States build and strengthen its infrastructure. Roads were built, railway lines laid, factories were built, and cities grew as populations were drawn from the countryside by the promise of jobs and increased social opportunities. Mined materials still play an important role in the strengthening of the country's

Miners exit an elevator that transports them daily between the surface and their underground workplace. Cramped, dark conditions are common in mining. It is certainly not a job for everyone.

infrastructure, thus creating unique job opportunities in the mining industry for many of its citizens.

TYPES OF MINING

When most people hear the term *mining,* they think of digging underground. But actually, there are two types of mining. While underground mining is certainly prevalent in North America, so too, is surface mining.

Underground mines use horizontal, vertical, or sloped openings. Drift mining uses paths cut horizontally into a hill to reach coal or ore deposits above water level. Vertical mining uses a very deep shaft dug close to or completely straight up and down to transport people and mining equipment to where the materials are. At various points off the shaft, miners create horizontal work areas, called levels, which allow them to reach mineral deposits more easily and efficiently. Slope mining is similar to shaft mining, except the entrance and

Blasting, using explosives, is a common activity in mining. Miners must constantly be aware of their surroundings due to the many perils they may encounter while working in this sector.

tunnels are sloped, not straight up and down, and the mine itself is not as deep.

Surface mining does not use shafts and tunnels. Instead, coal and mineral deposits are reached by digging through top layers of soil and rock only. The result is usually a large hole or pit. Quarries are an example of this type of open-pit mining, where they collect rock, stone, and gravel. Open-pit mining may also be used to gather certain minerals, such as copper. Other surface mining techniques include stripping away land over the deposit site layer by layer and blowing the tops off mountains to get to coal underneath.

THE TOP TAPPED RESOURCES

North America is rich in minerals that can be processed and manufactured to create construction materials used to build infrastructure. In the United States, these include iron ore, copper, nickel, and feldspar. Iron ore is crucial in the production of steel. Copper is used in electrical wiring components and tubing, while nickel-plating is sometimes used in plumbing pipes and valves because it helps prevent corrosion. Several different minerals are grouped under the name feldspar, which mixes with super-heated, melted sand to create glass.

Canada is among the top producers of the mineral potash, which is also used in the manufacture of glass. Canadian mines also supply large amounts of nickel, as well as the metals niobium (used to strengthen steel without adding a lot of weight), aluminum, tungsten, and graphite.

There are also several coal mines in North America; twenty-six of the fifty US states and four Canadian provinces support coal-mining operations. Coal is a fossil fuel that not only acts as a source of energy by generating electricity, but it

DRILLING VS. MINING

Two other types of fossil fuels, oil and gas, are popular heat and energy sources. As such, they are also considered important elements of a thriving infrastructure. Another similarity with coal is that these materials are extracted from beneath the earth's surface. It takes a great deal of time for exploration of oil and natural gas reserves, just as it does when trying to open a coal or mineral mine.

However, drilling is the extraction method for oil and gas, not mining. Instead of large shafts and tunnels that can accommodate many workers and large machinery, as in mining, drilling involves making small holes in the earth and the use of liquid or pressure to push oil and gas out of their resting places. In general, because most oil and natural gas are located far beneath the layers of rock that contain minerals or coal, drilling reaches deeper down than the average mine—where it would be next to impossible to send work crews.

is also involved in the processes that create steel and cement. Lightweight carbon-fiber construction materials are also made using coal.

Rock, sand, clay, and gravel are also precious commodities when building infrastructure. These things are used to create asphalt, which is crucial to creating modern roads and highways, as well as building materials such as

Vehicles wind their way up the twisting roads that lead down to a mine. Much of the mining industry exists far away from major city centers and towns.

concrete, plaster, and bricks. When shaped and polished, rocks may also be used as building materials in their fairly raw form. Mining for these materials is largely done in the ground, rather than underground.

BEFORE AND AFTER MINING

Turning coal, minerals, and metals into products used for infrastructure begins with exploration. Geoscientists help companies determine the best locations for mines during the exploration phase. They test soil and rock samples to determine what minerals are be present at a site. Scientists may also measure gravitational fields to see how different rocks are distributed, which provides clues as to which types of minerals may be present deep underground. Measuring the magnetic field helps them find mineral deposits buried closer to the surface. Exploration can take months or even years to complete.

Some materials, such as coal, come out of the ground pretty much in a usable form. Many minerals and metals, however, have other substances mixed in with the extracted material that must be removed. This mixed material is referred to as ore. Once the ore is extracted, it is taken to a plant where chemicals are added to separate the minerals from other materials in a process known as milling. Smelting breaks down the minerals even further through extreme heat; refining purifies the smelting end product into its purest usable form.

MINING HOT SPOTS

As numerous geologic surveys and the length of time it takes for exploration will attest, not every location is suitable for mining. There are several US states and Canadian provinces that hold large deposits of certain kinds of minerals and other mined materials. For instance, there are twenty-six states where coal mining is performed. Each year, Wyoming produces more coal than the next four—West Virginia, Kentucky, Pennsylvania, and Illinois—combined. In Canada, two western provinces have the largest coal deposits: Alberta and British Columbia. Saskatchewan and Nova Scotia have a few coal mines as well.

Mining for metal ore is big in Minnesota, Michigan, and Utah in the United States. In addition to coal, Saskatchewan supports metal ore mining operations. Ontario, Quebec, and Labrador reportedly have plenty of ore reserves as well.

Sand, stone, and gravel, known collectively in the mining trade as construction aggregates, can be found in numerous locations across North America. The top producers of these materials depend on which type of material is being mined.

WHO'S HIRING

The mining industry is not quite as thriving as it once was, but there are still jobs to be had in this sector. Data released by the US National Institute for Occupational Safety and Health for 2015 shows that nearly 33,000 active mines were operating

in the United States. The overwhelming majority of those were surface operations, with less than 5 percent reporting as underground mines.

As of 2015, coal mining and stone quarrying employed the most workers in the United States, at slightly more than 68,400 and 67,000 employees, respectively. Metal ore mining accounted for almost 41,500 jobs in that same time frame. Sand and gravel operations came in at more than 34,700 employees, and nonmetal ore mining companies hired some 26,000 workers that year.

Industry employment numbers for Canada were more broad-based. The Mining Association of Canada has reported that more than 373,000 people nationwide were working in the mining industry. That figure encompasses extraction, production, and manufacturing jobs. The association's website declares, "Mining is one of Canada's most important economic sectors and a major job creator."

CHAPTER TWO

SKILLED MINING JOBS

M any jobs in the mining sector do not require a four-year college degree. This does not mean that the people who perform these tasks are not skilled laborers. A lot of the skills required of those who work in mines and quarries revolve around how to operate various machines that, quite literally, do a lot of the "heavy lifting" in modern mines. There are technical colleges that give students hands-on training in running this equipment. For most miners, however, they learn on the job.

REAL OPERATORS

The first job title people associate with mining is, of course, miner. Those miners who work in quarries may be called quarriers. In years gone by, miners largely used pickaxes and shovels to extract coal, minerals, and stone from deposits beneath the surface. Today, they take advantage of machines that help them extract materials and transport

These workers don hard hats and face masks to man a drilling rig. They are digging for fluorite (also known as fluorspar), a mineral used in many commercial industrial and chemical processes.

them out of the mines. Their job titles may reflect the type of machine each miner controls or operates. Other names for underground miners include bore mine operator and continuous mining machine operator.

Miners are in the business of extracting the materials for infrastructure uses. They also produce minerals for commercial uses, such as additives in cosmetics and cleaning products; precious metals, such as gold and silver; and gemstones (diamonds, rubies). To get at these items, they use equipment that helps automate the process quite a bit. Typically, miners work in shifts.

In underground mining, miners operate continuous mining machines by remote control. Strong metal spikes, or teeth, connected to a huge cylinder scrape away everything in a machine's path as it rumbles through mine work areas. Coal and ore are then collected and sent on conveyor belts to be processed. Other machines operated by miners include longwall shears, which make the initial openings in underground mine "rooms."

Operating such heavy equipment involves more than pushing a button. Miners must first position these machines so that they cut and scrape in the most effective and productive manner. They also monitor the position and speed of the machines as they extract coal and other materials. Cleaning out clogged teeth and doing routine maintenance on these cutting monsters also is part of the job. They also install timber, roof supports, and casings, which form the framework that supports mine tunnels and make sure that mines are not in danger of buckling or collapsing as the machines excavate. Miners help

keep underground work areas well ventilated so that workers receive fresh air from the outside.

Machines are used in quarries as well, but nothing like the continuous mining machines used underground. By and large, pit miners operate excavators, cranes, mechanical drills, and other construction-like equipment, as well as stone graders and rock crushers. They may also rely on tools like jackhammers to extract stone and gravel from work sites.

EDUCATION AND TRAINING

Individuals who want to work as miners must be at least eighteen years old and able to pass a drug test. Employers looking to hire miners or quarriers typically want candidates to prove that they have graduated from high school. In addition, taking classes at a college that has programs in mining and technology will familiarize someone with the industry. An associate or bachelor's degree from a college or university is not a requirement for these types of jobs. What may be expected, however, is experience. On-the-job training is perhaps the most common way to learn the ropes.

Some companies are willing to hire individuals for menial, or less interesting, jobs at a mining site, such as working in a company office or cleaning equipment, while they learn the trade. Becoming an assistant to miners running the heavy equipment is another way to learn while working. Sometimes apprentice miners use their time as assistants or helpers to earn special licenses to operate trucks and other heavy vehicles on the job site. Mining employees also take safety classes throughout their careers.

While still in high school, prospective miners should concentrate on classes in the sciences (particularly geology) and math. Classes where students use a computer to perform tasks and operate machinery also are helpful, as is joining a robotics club.

A miner operates a process control panel. New remote technologies, increasingly powered by the internet, are an integral part of modern mining.

Holding any type of job while finishing high school makes a person more appealing than someone who has no work experience. But working at a construction site, during the

HARD WORK

Anyone who wants to work as a miner should be prepared to face some pretty tough working conditions. Miners better not be claustrophobic, because mine shafts, tunnels, and rooms are relatively small and cramped. Despite being ventilated, underground mines have poor air quality, which can lead to serious health problems.

Quarriers and pit miners work out in the fresh air, but that can have its own drawbacks. There is little protection from the heat, cold, and rain at these work sites, so miners and quarriers work a full day through all kinds of weather. Of course, when the weather is nice, being outside works to their advantage.

Miners also are on their feet throughout their shifts, and they are frequently required to do heavy lifting and other physical tasks. Yet those who can deal with such tricky conditions are rewarded with decent pay and the satisfaction of a job well done.

summer or through an internship in high school, is an excellent way to get a jump-start in the field.

WHAT THE FUTURE HOLDS

The Bureau of Labor Statistics (BLS) indicates that people who hold jobs as miners make a very good living wage, both hourly and when measured by annual salary. Unfortunately, the same source, as well as several industry associations, predicts that mining can be a tough field to enter. In fact, the BLS reports that mining jobs are on the decline in the United States. Openings for mining machine operators, have posted negative growth rates in recent years. Still, the need for materials to build infrastructure should continue well into the future. Jobs in certain mining sectors could rebound as infrastructure needs demand. Also, more positions could open up as miners age-out, retire, or switch fields.

WHAT A BLAST!

Mines and quarries are not made by digging and cutting alone. Often, explosives are used to loosen or blast away layers of dirt, rock, and other materials. This practice is most commonly used in pit or surface mining, but calculated explosions are also used in underground mines. The person who handles the explosives is sometimes called an ordnance worker, but more often simply is referred to as a blaster.

Employees gather in preparation for a round of explosives testing at an outdoor lab run by Axpro Research, a company specializing in blast experiments aimed to better improve the use of explosives in mining.

Simply put, blasters blow stuff up. But they do so in a controlled way that leads to greater access to mined materials. To perform their jobs properly and safely, blasters must know what types of explosives to use in certain situations, how much to use, and where detonations should take place to achieve the best results. They must also know how deep they should drill the holes into which the explosives are placed. Different patterns of multiple blast holes may be necessary to clear large areas. Misplacement of dynamite and other explosives can be ineffective or cause parts of the mine to collapse.

Blasters are responsible for handling the explosives they use in the course of their work. That means they are in charge of storing and transporting hazardous materials. They also make sure they have enough explosives on hand to complete a job, which means taking inventory and ordering whatever else is needed.

EDUCATION, TRAINING, AND CERTIFICATION

As far as formal education goes, blasters, like most mine workers, only need to have graduated from high school to be considered for employment. Because of the danger involved in this job, blasters generally have to undertake explosives training, which leads to earning a blasting permit or license. Requirements for licensure vary by US state and Canadian province, but typically prospective blasters must pass a written exam covering knowledge of explosives types and procedures, as well as health and safety issues involved in the field. Proof that a person knows how to safely detonate explosives may also be required.

High school math classes help those who would like to become blasters. Knowledge of chemistry could help such individuals pack, or prepare, the explosive charges. A background in computer science or a related discipline is beneficial since it can help prospective blasters learn to operate equipment on the job site.

A FUTURE IN MINING

While blasting is not a rapidly growing career field, at least it is not on the decline, as are several other mining jobs. Blasting is a very important part of surface mining, so there should always be a demand for these types of workers, at least to some degree. Exactly how much demand, however, remains to be seen. The Bureau of Labor Statistics estimates that there will be approximately 1,900 job openings for all explosives workers, including mining blasters, through 2024. Therefore, competition for blaster jobs could be pretty fierce. Candidates who are diligent about remaining current on their licensure, receive additional training recommended by their employer and the state in which they work, and have a squeaky-clean safety record are most likely to stand out from the crowd and land available jobs.

MINING TECHNICIANS

Among those considered skilled workers in this industry arc mining technicians. These individuals support the work of geologists and engineers. Their workload is more academic and laboratory based, versus the more strictly manual labor of miners and blasters. There is another difference between these jobs and those that involve actual extraction of materials. Holding a high school diploma alone will not get one in the door as an entry-level tech. The nature of a mining technician's work requires at least an associate degree from a reputable college or university.

Also called geological technicians, mining technicians are part of a mine's entire life. During exploration, they work to develop mines by helping to conduct soil and rock sampling at prospective sites. Working in laboratories out in the field, they test samples to see what minerals might be present underground and where precisely the richest lodes or veins might be. During a mine's production phase, mining technicians may perform similar tests to determine the value of the product being extracted. They may also go down into underground mines to check the air quality.

Mining technicians primarily work with geologists, but they can also help mining engineers perform their duties. Engineers in this field determine the safest and most effective way to build and run a mine. Based on sampling and testing, mining technicians write reports and give input regarding how to best complete these tasks while maintaining the mine's structural integrity and productivity. When performing engineering-related tasks such as writing reports, mining

A teacher demonstrates the use of a simple tool in a mechanical engineering lab. Some of the higher-paid and more specialized jobs in mining require more than on-the-job training.

engineers may work out of an office instead of underground, in the field, or inside a lab.

FORMAL EDUCATION

As mentioned, mining technicians are expected to have an undergraduate degree. The minimum qualifications require an associate degree, which normally takes two years to complete. Some colleges have degree programs or even entire departments focused on geology, other geosciences, or engineering. Still others offer specialized programs leading to an associate degree. For instance, the University of Alaska offers an associate of applied science degree in process technology, which includes mining. Also, there are technical and vocational schools that offer two-year degrees in mining and related disciplines.

Finally, much like their less skilled counterparts in the mining industry, mining technicians also benefit from receiving on-the-job training in addition to formal education. Many college students can work while they study through internships. Then there is even more opportunity to gain new skills, as well as an accompanying chance for workplace advancement, by taking an entry-level job and getting on-the-job training.

High school students can prepare for taking college-level courses and eventual work as mining technicians by emphasizing math, chemistry, and physics classes in their student workload. Because they need to communicate clearly and precisely on the job, future mining technicians would do well to also take courses in speech and technical writing while still in high school.

A FUTURE FOR MINING TECHNICIANS

Experts predict that the employment outlook for geological technicians is rosy. Employment numbers are expected to rise through 2026, with growth occurring faster than normal for positions within any field. Thanks in no small part to their having a postsecondary degree, mining technicians also command a decent starting salary, and the salaries only go up once individuals log a few years of experience on the job.

Of course, a career as a mining technician is not exactly a burgeoning field. A fairly limited number of positions come open over the course of a year. Yet there is good news when it comes to job security. Geological techs are also in demand in the oil and natural gas sectors. Because a mining technician's skill set can be applied in a number of related career fields, these individuals may have better prospects for employment even if finding work with a mining company falls through.

CHAPTER THREE

MANUAL LABORERS AND HELPERS

*B*ecause employers in the field value experience, most mine workers begin their careers by taking entry-level positions, where they can acquire vital on-the-job training. In the trade, people in these positions are manual laborers and helpers. Mining laborers are those who perform manual labor and construction-related tasks, such as shoveling, breaking up rocks, and loading trucks. Instead of large, remote-controlled machines, these workers are more likely to use manual tools or small power tools, such as jackhammers and chisels. Helpers are junior-level employees who work as assistants to more seasoned professionals.

ROCK SPLITTERS

Blasters clear tons of rock and create entire shelves, or levels, of a quarry mining material at a time. As one might imagine, blowing up solid rock from quarry walls does not yield stones that are ready-made for building infrastructure and other construction purposes.

This mechanical digger is breaking up rock ore in an underground gold mine. Knowing one's way around heavy equipment is a must in this industry.

Enter workers called rock splitters. Using sturdy hand tools (although jackhammers are also incorporated) and physical strength, these workers break apart massive slabs of rock into more manageable and useful pieces.

The job description for rock splitters can be found in the job title itself—they literally split rocks. The method used to do this has been around for centuries, although modern rock splitters working in quarries have added a new twist or two.

Stone forms when enormous pressure forces soil, minerals, and other natural materials together into a hardened clump.

Traces of where these elements have come together form a stone's grain. Rock splitting begins with workers examining large slabs of stone to figure out their grain patterns. They want to split with the grain, not against or across it, for the easiest separation and the smoothest line. Next, they draw a chalk outline on the stone, to make sure they get the right size and shape, and that they are splitting the rock into straight lines.

Once the area to be split is marked, rock splitters drill small holes along the outline, a few inches apart. This step was once accomplished using manual metal drills and a sledgehammer. Today, workers use a jackhammer. Metal wedges are placed inside each hole between two thin metal braces or shims, called "feathers" in the trade. Rock splitters pound the wedges and feathers deep into the rock, eventually causing it to split.

As one might imagine, rock splitting is hard physical labor. Bending over a rock while swinging a heavy sledgehammer for eight hours day takes stamina and plenty of upper body strength. Rock splitters wear special gear that protects their ears from the noise of drilling and hammering, their eyes from bits of stone that may fly loose, and their feet from toppling stone halves after larger pieces are split, as well as whacks from sledgehammers that might accidentally miss their mark.

STRAIGHT OUT OF SCHOOL

Graduation from high school is the only formal education requirement someone has to meet to become a rock splitter. Even though there is not much emphasis on book learning,

Besides one's technical skills, the willingness to spend long amounts of time underground and away from the sun is another major consideration when considering a job in mining.

rock splitting—done properly—is definitely a learned skill. Rock splitters, like most mine and quarry laborers, receive their training from professionals in their field who have been on the job for a few years.

Yet, classroom learning also has its place in a career path. Math teaches how to figure the depth and possible angles needed when drilling holes and placing wedges. Earth science and geology help people identify the various types of stones and their physical properties, such as density and breaking point. Vocational courses in mechanics, metalworking, or construction can add an extra layer to job preparedness, as they prepare candidates to handle and maintain equipment and tools.

ROCK SPLITTERS: JOB PROSPECTS

The outlook for rock splitters is pretty average for the mining field, meaning tremendous growth in this area is not expected. In fact, experts say data shows employment for this job title is on the decline. Virtually every quarry hires rock splitters, but the number of splitters hired overall each year in the US quarrying sector is limited.

More bad news follows the trend in mining toward increased mechanization. Machines perform tasks more quickly and efficiently than humans using traditional means. As improved tools and automated machinery are developed in this field, fewer tradespeople will be needed.

People who have or can learn the skills involved in being a rock splitter may be able to find work if they are willing to look outside of quarry employment. Sometimes their talent and training may be need on construction sites during infrastructure building and overhauling.

Rock splitting is not a very lucrative career—at least not at first. Hourly pay for entry-level positions may not be much above minimum wage. But with experience, these workers can earn a middle-class salary.

MINE SHUTTLE CAR OPERATORS

In the beginning days of mining, animal-drawn carts or wagons were used to transport miners and extracted materials to and from the depths of underground mines. Other methods, such as steam-powered trams or cable cars, also served this purpose as time went by. Nowadays, moving materials is the job of mine shuttle car operators, who drive electric or diesel trollies.

Mine shuttle operators do more than drive. After correctly positioning the shuttle cars under loading spouts, they operate the conveyor system that loads materials, monitoring the process to make sure the weight of materials is evenly distributed. If it is not, the shuttle could stall or overturn as it makes its way up inclines or around tight corners. Because noise and distance may be factors that complicate the loading process, mine shuttle operators incorporate a system of hand signals to let others know when their cars are ready for loading or completely full. They are in charge of the unloading process as well.

Mine shuttle operators also act as mechanics, servicing and repairing their vehicles, sometimes on the fly. Many also take on the responsibility of measuring and weighing transported material.

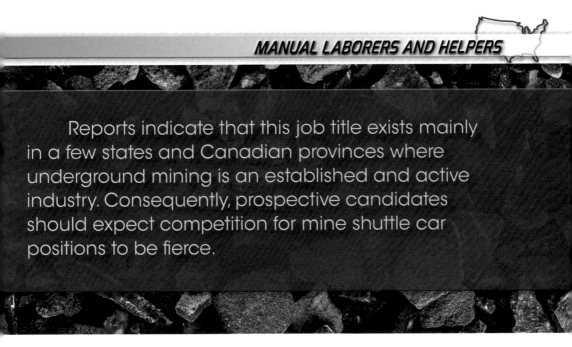

Reports indicate that this job title exists mainly in a few states and Canadian provinces where underground mining is an established and active industry. Consequently, prospective candidates should expect competition for mine shuttle car positions to be fierce.

EXTRACTION HELPERS

To obtain most skilled mining jobs, entry-level employees first go through a kind of initiation process where they learn from more experienced workers. Those who are training to learn a specific skilled mining trade are referred to in general as helpers. Drillers, blasters, roof bolters, and mining machine operators all make use of having helpers on hand at mining sites.

Extraction helpers assist senior extraction workers to complete the many tasks associated with their jobs. Typically, helpers start off slow, performing work that requires the least amount of experience or skill. In the beginning few weeks and months of work, these tasks may include cleaning up after, carting around supplies for, and watching the professionals they are helping. Throughout their time as helpers, they should find themselves performing any number of tasks—whatever it takes to keep their supervisory worker happy and the entire mine running as smoothly as possible.

Workers in the foreground perform landscape surveys. Behind them, a giant electric shovel loads copper ore into a truck that can haul hundreds of tons of materials.

Helpers' responsibilities grow the longer they are on the job. Eventually, blaster helpers might be tasked with drilling blasting holes, then placing explosives in the holes alongside, and under the supervision of, a senior blaster. Continuous mining machine operator helpers would be charged with monitoring the performance of the machine or cleaning debris from the cylinder's teeth that is slowing down its progress and productivity. In general, helpers of all kinds maintain machines, keep track of and supply tools, and help load and unload equipment that travels between the surface and the interior environment of mines and quarries. More advanced helpers may act as backups, rather than assistants, to the extraction workers who are their supervisors.

Since many skilled mining professionals only require a high school diploma for employment, it stands to reason that their helpers would need to meet no more than the same criterion. Sure enough, a person can get an extraction helper job by graduating from high school or receiving his or her General Equivalency Diploma (GED).

What should these workers study in school to prepare them for their careers? That depends on the area for which they are acting as a helper. But while the particulars may be up for grabs, there are still the stand-by subjects connected with so many mining jobs, namely math and science.

The growth rate for extraction helper jobs through 2026 is much better than that for the positions they are helping. This could be because the mining industry is looking to incoming helpers to fill positions vacated by workers who have retired or found jobs in other fields. Plus, helpers generally have the least

This dump truck is one of many attractions at the CC&V mine, a mining operation with tours open to the public in Victor, Colorado, run by Newmont Mining Corporation in collaboration with the Victor Lowell Thomas Museum.

experience and skills on a mining site, and therefore they are assigned a number of different tasks, so they can learn the job they hope to get from every angle. Any type of business or work site is happy to hire people who can perform tasks that may not be glamorous but are crucial to getting the job done. Helpers also get paid less than more experienced extraction workers. That alone could make them very attractive to employers.

CHAPTER FOUR

THE LOGGING INDUSTRY

Logging is the process of harvesting, or cutting down, trees for their wood. Several uses for this lumber pertain to building infrastructure. These include the use of wood in structural building, particularly in US and Canadian houses. In fact, British Columbia passed the Wood First Act in 2009, which requires that all new building or expansion projects whose construction is publicly funded by the province use wood as the main building material. Wood and wood products are also valuable as a natural, renewable source of energy.

Logging could be described as the first infrastructure-related occupation in the history of the United States. Colonists felled trees to build their houses and other structures. They also cleared land of trees to create farming fields. Lumber was also exported for shipbuilding and other wooden products, a trade that thrived well into the nineteenth century. Expansion westward, to land that was heavily forested, moved logging centers from the East and the Midwest to the Pacific Northwest, where it still continues today. Lumber has also been a staple of the Canadian economy since that time as well.

This mountainside has been cleared of most of its trees and vegetation. Clear-cutting is just one way of managing lumber supplies in a given region, and the practice itself can often be problematic for the environment.

Clearly, logging as a profession is deeply rooted in North American culture. The industry has certainly had its ups and downs, the latter coming during periods of shrinking supply, arboreal disease, and concerns over the state of the environment. Yet, the logging trade still holds a strong place as a career path that affects a nation's infrastructure.

TYPES OF LOGGING

There are several ways to harvest timber. In forested areas, mature trees often protect young saplings from hazards that might cut short their life cycle. The shelterwood system makes sure that older trees remain areas being logged to ensure that the younger are protected. The canopy created by the leaves of taller trees can also benefit growing trees that prefer shade. Eventually, the older trees may be harvested, but only after the seedlings are able to make it on their own.

Selection cutting is the process by which specific trees are chosen for harvesting. Trees may be selected because an order has been placed for a certain kind of wood. Or they may be selected because the trees are almost past their prime, meaning their wood is deteriorating and soon will no longer be strong and useful. This method should not be confused with selective cutting, in which the trees that have the most value in the timber marketplace are harvested, no matter their age.

Clear-cutting involves the harvesting of all the trees in a given forested area. This is a relatively quick and effective method of logging, allowing for high yields of wood at one time. This method also gives landowners the chance to choose the types of trees they grow without having to rely on what nature sows on its own. For instance, landowners may choose to plant trees that produce wood that is highly valued or in demand in their area, which will earn them more money when the trees are harvested.

Two coworkers examine a pile of harvested logs. There are many things to check even after trees have been felled.

There is a downside to clear-cutting. Environmentalists and others criticize it because it destroys the habitats of trees, animals, and other living things. Clearcutting also puts the land at greater risk for erosion because there are few to no tree roots or other vegetation to help anchor the soil in place. Trees are a renewable resource, meaning more can be grown to replace those that are harvested, yet it takes years for trees to grow to the desired useful maturity.

Felled logs need to be transported to lumber mills and other destinations. This must be done no matter the weather, or how remote the logging site is.

TIMBER FOR INFRASTRUCTURE

Timber has many uses within the larger field of infrastructure construction and maintenance. It is used to repair and fortify wood bridges, as well as steel bridges with wooden decks. Bridge supports, such as railroad trestles, can be made of timber, and the ties that hold railroad rails in place also are largely made of wood.

MOVING UP IN THE WORLD

When building skyscrapers, construction workers use steel to frame these towering buildings. Steel provides the rigid strength necessary to withstand high winds at great heights, as well as the pressure from the weight of multiple stories. That is why wood is largely used to construct homes and other low-rise buildings. However, a relatively new type of wood processing is helping timber "rise" to the challenge of multistory building.

Cross-laminated timber (CLT) can be thought of as the big brother version of plywood. Large wood panels are laminated to one another in such a way as to strengthen a resulting larger, thicker panel. In construction, using CLT is easier to handle than heavy, bulky steel bars, and the material provides good heat and sound insulation. The cost of CLT is about the same as other materials.

Several multistory buildings in Europe have used CLT, as well as a student dormitory in British Columbia and a condominium in Quebec, both in Canada. The United States has generally not embraced the CLT trend for high-rise building, but the market for this type of construction may improve in the near future.

The most common uses of timber for infrastructure are the building of homes and other low buildings. Softwood timber, such as pine and cedar, is the most commonly used wood in home building. This kind of wood is less dense and therefore is easy to work with in construction: nails and saws go through softwood efficiently. Softwood timber also is commonly used to create plywood, a processed wood product wherein several thin wood sheets are glued together to form a thicker, stronger sheet. Plywood is often found in the beams, braces, ceilings, and walls of homes.

Hardwood is used most often in making furniture, flooring, and decorative or utilitarian (cabinets, doors) features inside homes. Some hardwood trees, such as birches, are used to manufacture plywood. Hardwood is also the wood that is typically burned as a fuel or heating source.

WHERE THE LOGS ARE

Unlike mining, which depends on finding sites containing coal, rock, and mineral deposits, logging can be done just about anywhere there are multiple acres of trees. As recently as 2014, North America accounted for more than a quarter of the world's timber production from commercial logging.

In the United States, logging operations are concentrated in the Northeast; throughout the Eastern seaboard states, particularly in New England and the Carolinas; across the South, from the Carolinas into Texas; and in the Pacific Northwest. Alaska is also home to commercial logging

A skidder moves a log in the woods. Modern logging technologies allow for smaller crews than used to be necessary in the nineteenth century, when labor-saving machines were cruder or had not been devised yet.

operations. Millions of forested acres exist in several provinces, particularly Alberta, British Columbia, Ontario, and Saskatchewan.

Forests throughout North America are a combination of privately and publicly owned land. Small plots of treed land and hundreds of acres overseen by corporations constitute private ownership. A country's federal government mainly owns public lands. Both types of owners hire loggers to work their land. Loggers can work as independent contractors or as employees of a logging company.

CHAPTER FIVE

CLIMB AND CUT

*T*hey used to be known as lumberjacks. The men—back when it was only men—who cut down trees to sell as timber lived in remote camps set up by their employers deep in the forests where they worked. They used axes and crosscut saws to cut into and fell trees.

How the times have changed. Today, the men—along with women, who hold approximately three percent of logging jobs in the country—who cut down trees for a living are more popularly known as loggers. Many loggers commute to the job site rather than living there, as logging camps are no longer the norm. Modern loggers may pick up an axe from time to time, but hand sawing has been replaced with gas-powered chainsaws. Even more advanced technology has arrived on the scene, making the harvesting of trees that much quicker and more efficient.

One thing has not changed, however. Loggers still work on crews, using teamwork to get the job done. The first step in the logging process is cutting down trees. The person who does this is called the feller. Cutting the limbs off a tree's trunk may be done by the feller or by another employee called a bucker.

A logger clambers up a tree trunk in Lakeside, Montana. Such physical work makes strength and endurance basic requirements for most of those working in logging.

FELLERS AND BUCKERS

There is some debate about whether the proper term is "fallers" or "fellers," but either way, these are the folks who bring down trees with a cut, a chop . . . and, of course, the buzz of a chainsaw. Fellers are classified by the tools that they use. Those that harvest using hand tools, such as axes and power saws, are referred to as hand or manual fellers. Modern technology has made its way deep into the woods with machines called harvesters, which can fell trees and process them into logs many times faster than hand fellers can. Usually, the larger logging operations, which need to process hundreds of acres of trees quickly and can afford the cost, own and use this type of equipment. Smaller operations and independent contractors mostly stick with hand felling.

Before felling a tree, fellers will assess the position, height, and growth angle of that tree, as well as those around it. They need to figure out where to make their cuts, how to get the tree to fall where they want, and have a path to safety in mind before beginning. Attention is paid to limbs of nearby trees that may come crashing down if knocked by the falling tree or change the direction of the fall.

Cuts are made in a certain order. The first is the downward-angled top cut, which determines the way the tree will fall. The undercut is made below that, angled so that a V-shaped notch is formed. Finally, fellers make a back cut, made on the opposite side of the other two cuts and meeting them where they intersect.

Once a tree is on the ground, buckers remove the top and the limbs and cut the timber into logs. Buckers use similar equipment as fellers do. In fact, sometimes fellers will include bucking in their job descriptions. Some loggers have been known to attempt bucking up in a tree, while it is still standing. This is not generally recommended, as it makes an already dangerous job even more hazardous.

BULLBUCK

Both fellers and the buckers come under the supervision of a manager called a bullbuck. People in this position make sure the harvesting operation is safe, direct cutting operations, and check to make sure work is being done properly. Bullbucks also have administrative duties, such as scheduling, interviewing, and training new workers; checking inventory; and ordering supplies. Even though they are in a supervisory position, bullbucks do not need any special educational requirements beyond a high school diploma, which most logging workers must possess. Fellers with several years of experience on the job may be promoted to the bullbuck position.

Harvester operators can fell and buck trees from the safety of the machine's cab. The harvester is equipped with a chainsaw, sharp blades for taking off limbs, and rollers to grasp the trunks, which allow the operator to better control the direction in which the cut tree falls. Some harvesters, called feller-bunchers, also collect the felled and delimbed trees so they can be transported to a clearing or a waiting truck. Harvester operators compare running these machines to a combination of driving a vehicle and working on a computer.

A tree is felled at a logging site run by Crook Logging of Groveland, California. This area of the Stanislaus National Forest near Yosemite National Park was damaged by the 2013 Rim Fire wildfire.

EXPERIENCE OVER EDUCATION

When it comes to a career as a feller or bucker, experience matters more than getting a formal education. A high school diploma is all the education required of a beginning logger. If a logger wanted to receive additional education in the field, he or she could take community college or tech school classes in forestry, which is a field related to logging. Forestry involves developing and caring for the world's forests, as well as the management of growing and harvesting timber.

THOUGHTS FROM THE PROS

Ted Simmon fells trees by hand. He likes the fact that he can earn good money as an independent contractor who finds his own work. Simmon learned the trade from his father. The following are excerpts from an interview with Simmon that appeared on the College Foundation of North Carolina website.

On learning how to be a feller: "You start learning tricks from the older fallers. ... The only way to learn is by doing. People can explain what a certain type of tree is like, but until you put your saw into it yourself, you're not sure what it will do."

Regarding safety: "A faller that thinks he knows everything is a faller that is going to get hurt."

Francois Allard also learned from more experienced loggers. He started driving a tractor for his family's logging business when he was seven, and worked his way up to being a feller. Today, he operates a feller-buncher. The following are excerpts from his portion of the same interview.

On salary and getting paid: "If we're short of work, there's no income. And that can be stressful."

On starting a logging career: "Come and talk to loggers. Ask if you can spend a few days at a camp and see how you like the lifestyle."

A logger feeds a log into a log-cutting bench and splitter. Workers need to take great care in their movements when dealing with the powerful machinery used in this industry.

Fellers and buckers receive training from more seasoned loggers. This is especially true for those who want to work as hand fellers. Harvester operators may need more practical training on how to work their machines. Forestry and logging organizations typically run logging training programs.

Jobs for fellers and buckers are expected to decline through 2026. The BLS expects a 7 percent decline for all logging positions, with 11 percent fewer openings for hand fellers. Part of the problem is that harvesters fell and buck trees much more quickly and efficiently than those who do these tasks by hand. Logging employers will need fewer hand fellers and buckers, and fewer harvester operators, too.

Falling demand for timber may also affect employment. Dwindling forest habitats and building slowdowns could decrease lumber sales. However, an uptick in the number of houses being built and increased use of products like cross-laminated timber could create more jobs for those who harvest the wood.

CHAPTER SIX

MOVE, MEASURE, AND MARK

*E*arly logging operations used horses and other animals to pull cut trees to sawmills where they were made into lumber. In today's commercial logging operations, machines have replaced animals. Additional advances in moving timber, such as high-lead and skyline logging—where logs were guided down mountain slopes or flown high above the ground on cable systems—have also benefitted from becoming more mechanized. So, too, have the men and women whose jobs revolve around these machines and mechanized cable transportation systems, known in the trade as rigging.

THE RIGGING CREW

Rigging crews take over a logging operation after trees have been cut. Harvested trees are moved from where they were felled to a landing—an area where the timber is put on trucks and taken to sawmills—via rigging methods. The timber can be moved on the ground by a skidder or through the air on a pulley system referred to as high-lead yarding. Jobs in this area of logging include choker setters, chasers, and rigging slingers.

This worker gets a log ready for the crane that will hoist it into place for processing at a lumber mill. Loggers are just part of the industry that begins in the woods and ends with new furniture and other products in homes and businesses.

ALL CHOKED UP

Choker setters position steel cables around felled trees. The choker is a nooselike loop of cabled wire that is wrapped around a thick section of a log or logs. Chokers are used both when logs are being dragged to the landing on the ground and when they are glided down on high leads overhead. Choker loops are adjustable so that they can fit different-sized loads. Choker setters are responsible for making sure that the loop is secure, so the log or logs do not slip loose while being transported. They also make sure that logs traveling from the harvesting site make it safely down the wires of high-lead rigging, reporting on their progress to the landing crew and ensuring that no one gets hit by a flying log.

Usually, there is more than one choker setter on each rigging crew team. Because they are dealing with distance, as well as a lot of noise from chainsaws and machinery, choker setters communicate with other members of the rigging crew using special, universally recognized hand signals.

UP FOR THE CHASE

Another group of workers detach the choker and release the logs. Chasers are so named because they "chase after" the logs that have arrived at landings to take off the rigging cables. They help tell rigging machine operators where the arriving logs should be placed, so there is little to no physical chasing involved. As with choker setters, chasers use nonverbal cues, including hand signs and whistle signals, to communicate with other crew members.

Once they unhook the choker cable, chasers clean up the delivered logs, removing anything that the bucker may have overlooked or missed. Some chasers mark the logs to indicate which ones are ready to be loaded on the truck. Chasers also attach logs to loader wires so that they can be positioned on a truck trailer bed for transport.

LOG HOOKERS

A job that is auxiliary to choke setters and chasers is log hooker. Logging operations located high up on mountain hillsides where dragging logs or even using high-lead rigging is not practical employ these workers. Instead, these operations rely on helicopters to move the logs from the cutting site to a landing. Log hookers attach a cable dropped from the helicopter securely to the choker. This is not a highly skilled job, nor does it require a college degree to accomplish. Yet the same crucial attention to detail and concern for safe transportation of logs required by choke setters and chasers are needed for the log hooker position.

A RIGGED JOB

Rigging slingers are supervisors who oversee the work of choker setters and chasers, as well as rigging machine operators. As such, they perform many of the same tasks as any supervisor would, such as directing the workflow, making sure there are enough workers to handle any given project, and overseeing the way each team member performs.

A timber crane moves several logs off a pile. Running cranes and other heavy equipment is another skill set that someone can be taught in the course of a logging career.

Rigging slingers are in charge of figuring out the order in which a stand of trees is to be harvested and letting everyone on the team know how the day is going to progress. The responsibility for huge logs being safely delivered to the landing lies with them. While choker setters and chasers help direct the safe movement of cut timber from their particular positions on site, they take their cues from the rigging slinger, who needs to ensure that everything is going as planned, from the harvesting site straight through to the landing. When necessary, these supervisors may perform the tasks assigned to any member of their crew.

As with so many others who choose a logging career, members of the rigging crew do not need a college education to find work. A practical education received on the job is much better preparation. This is especially true of rigging slingers, who typically log at least five years of time working as fellers or choker setters before they can be considered for this supervisory position. Proving oneself at a current job is the best way to get a promotion in logging.

Logging, as a whole, is not an expanding field. The demand for choker setters, chasers, and rigging slingers is projected to be weak for the foreseeable future. Employment will depend on how many workers retire or otherwise leave the field, thereby creating openings. A surge in lumber or paper product sales could boost employment numbers as well.

HEAVY EQUIPMENT OPERATORS

Logging has become largely mechanized, but the career field is far from automated. Laborers are needed to operate the heavy equipment. In addition to harvesters—as well as an assortment of trucks, bulldozers, backhoes, and excavators one might expect to find on such a worksite—there are other machines specific to logging that need experienced drivers and controllers. Skidders and yarders are among the most prominent pieces of heavy equipment used by logging operations.

Rigging slingers act as managers on a logging site, overseeing every worker who has a hand in getting timber from where it is felled to the landing.

ON THE SKIDS

A skidder combines the jobs of a tractor, bulldozer, and all-terrain vehicle. Skidders are equipped with a winch, around the drum of which a length of steel cable is wound. At the other end of the cable is the choker noose. When the choker is secured to a log, the winch reels in the timber so that the skidder can drag it to the landing. Skidder operators are charged with driving the vehicle through rough forest terrain without losing their loads or injuring fellow workers and the remaining forest environment along the way. They are also at the controls of the winch.

Adding attachments, such as blades, to the front of a skidder allows the operator to perform other tasks, including clearing vegetation, logging debris, and rocks from paths and roads. Skidder operators work closely with choker setters and chasers. They must learn the same hand signals used by these other team members to properly communicate the movement of their machines. Maintenance and simple repairs to their equipment are also their responsibility.

WORK BY THE YARD

Yarder operators work from a logging site's landing, where the machine can remain stabilized on a flat surface, rather than on a hillside where trees are being harvested. Yarders resemble cranes, with an operator cab and a tall tower that may be either stationary or mobile. Mobile yarders are often referred to as swing yarders. Inside the cab are hand and foot controls, which allow the yarder operator to control the machine's winches, which allow them to set up, position, and move high-lead rigging cables.

Logs attached by chokers travel along the cable rigging using a high-lead system. In skyline logging, the yarder operator guides a small machine attached to the cable, called a carriage, which has a retractable wire that attaches to logs via a choker. Yarder operators may also control a hinged mechanical claw called a grapple to grab logs instead of having a choker attached.

The yarder operator communicates with choker setters, chasers, and other logging crew members via radio, hand signals, and a system of horn beeps and whistles. Keeping the machine in good working order is also on the yarder operator's to-do list.

Logging equipment operators control heavy machinery that grabs logs and loads them onto trucks. They rely on signals and horns to keep nearby workers on the ground safe.

TRAINING AND OUTLOOK

Once again, hands-on experience on a logging crew trumps a traditional education. Prospective skidder and yarder operators are typically first employed as choker setters or chasers—the types of workers that these heavy equipment operators work with on a daily basis. An apprenticeship under an experienced machine operator may also be required, or at least highly recommended. Proven mechanical ability, particularly operating or maintaining other types of vehicles or heavy machinery, also works in a candidate's favor.

According to the Bureau of Labor Statistics, few logging equipment operator positions will be opening up in the years ahead. The good news, though, is that the mechanical skills required for these positions tend to translate pretty well into the operation of other heavy construction equipment. Therefore, finding a job outside of the logging field may be a possible temporary measure for these workers.

- **What They Do:** Mining workers are in the business of extracting materials from the earth, such as mineral ores and slabs of stone. These materials are processed to make a variety of products, including uses in building and construction. Logging workers harvest thousands of acres of forests each year. The timber they harvest provides the raw material for many consumer goods and industrial products.

- **Work Environment:** Mining and logging are physically demanding trades and can be dangerous. Mining workers toil deep underground or in pits dug out of the ground. Logging crews spend their entire time outdoors, sometimes in poor weather and often in isolated areas.

- **Education and Training:** Most mining and logging workers have a high school diploma. On-the-job training prepares them for the work environment and the operation of various machinery. Those who wish to advance in these fields to the managerial level may want to consider taking technical school or college-level courses, even getting an associate degree.

- **Earnings:** The pay scale for jobs in these fields is solidly in middle-class territory. As in other career fields, entry-level jobs pay less than those requiring more experience. Depending on the company and the position, mining and logging employees are paid either an hourly wage or an annual salary.

- **Employment Outlook:** Overall employment of mining and logging workers is projected to decline through 2026. However, there will be a need to replace workers who retire or leave the occupation.

GLOSSARY

apprentice Someone who learns a trade or type of work from a more experienced worker.

arboreal Of or related to trees.

canopy A cover created by leaves and needles of upper tree limbs in a forest.

contractor Someone who independently enters into an agreement to complete work for another.

criterion The standard by which something can be judged or a decision made.

erosion Wearing away.

extraction Pulling something out of a larger body.

laminated Made up of many layers of material that are bound together.

ore Source minerals that contain valuable material, such as metals or minerals.

quarry An open-pit mine containing stone, slate, and similar materials.

rigging A network of lines and chains used to move heavy objects from one spot to another.

shaft A mine opening that goes deep underground.

shim A thin piece of metal that fills a hole space and supports a wedge during rock splitting.

skidder A logging vehicle that drags logs from the cutting area to a landing.

stamina Physical or mental strength that lets someone participate for a long time.

structural Having to do with the physical makeup of something.

utilitarian Something that serves a specific useful purpose.

ventilated Describes a place where fresh air is circulated.

winch A machine used to move large, heavy items using cable, rope, or wire wrapped around a drum.

yarder A piece of heavy equipment that allows for the movement of logs along cable rigging systems.

Great Lakes Timber Professionals Association (GLTPA)
3243 Golf Course Road
PO Box 1278
Rhinelander, WI 54501
(715) 282-5828
Email: info@gltpa.org
Website: http://gltpa.org
GLTPA is a nonprofit organization proud to represent forest
  industry members in Michigan and Wisconsin and is
  committed to leading the forest products industry in
  sustainable forest management.

National Mining Association (NMA)
101 Constitution Avenue NW, Suite 500 East
Washington, DC 20001
(202) 463-2600
Website: https://nma.org
Twitter: @nationalmining
Facebook: @NationalMining
NMA is the only national trade organization that represents
  the interests of mining before Congress, the administration,
  federal agencies, the judiciary, and the media.

Sustainable Forest Management in Canada/Forest in Mind
580 Booth Street, 7th Floor
Ottawa, Ontario K1A 0E4
Canada
(613) 462-4987
Email: forestinmind@sfmcanada.org

Website: https://www.sfmcanada.org/en
Forest in Mind is a project of Sustainable Forest Management
    in Canada, and it hopes to position Canada as a
    world leader in sustainable forest management and
    environmental stewardship to protect and enhance market
    access for Canadian forest products.

Timber Harvesting Magazine
PO Box 2268
Montgomery, AL 36102
(800) 669-5613
Website: http://www.timberharvesting.com
Facebook: @timberharvesting
Twitter: @timberharvmag
Published six times a year, *Timber Harvesting* covers jobs and
    general industry news in the logging business.

United Mine Workers of America (UMWA)
18354 Quantico Gateway Drive, Suite 200
Triangle, VA 22172
(703) 291-2400
info@umwa.org
Website: http://umwa.org
Facebook and Instagram: @umwaunion
Twitter: @mineworkers
The United Mine Workers of America is a North American
    labor union known for representing the interests of coal
    miners, along with workers in other industries.

Women in Mining Canada (WIMC)
157 Adelaide Street West, Suite 511
Toronto, ON M5H 4E7
Canada
info@wimcanada.org
Website: http://wimcanada.org
Facebook: @wimcanada
Twitter: @wim_canada
Women in Mining Canada (WIMC) is a national nonprofit
organization formed in 2009 focused on advancing
the interests of women in the minerals exploration and
mining sectors.

Women in Mining Education Foundation
PO Box 260246
Lakewood, CO 80226
(866) 537-9694
Email: wimef@womeninmining.org
Website: http://www.womeninmining.org
Twitter: @WomenInMining
The Women In Mining Education Foundation is a nonprofit
educational organization that educates others about the
importance of the minerals industry.

FOR FURTHER READING

Brannigan, Grace. *Hey, Mr. Logger*. East Jewett, NY: Questor Books, 2015.

Garbe, Suzanne. *Killer Jobs!: History's Most Dangerous Jobs*. North Mankato, MN: Capstone Press, 2014.

Gardner, Jane P., and Richard Garratt. *Timber and Forest Products*. Broomall, PA: Mason Crest, 2016.

Gordon, Nick. *Coal Miner*. Minneapolis, MN: Bellwether Media, 2013.

Henry, Claire. *The World's Deadliest Jobs*. New York, NY: PowerKids Press, 2014.

James, Dawn. *Turning Trees into Paper*. New York, NY: Cavendish Square Publsihing, 2015.

Linde, Barbara M. *Strip Mining*. New York, NY: Gareth Stevens Publishing, 2014.

Marshall, Pam. *From Tree to Paper*. Minneapolis, MN: Lerner Publications, 2013.

Marsico, Katie. *What's It Like to Live Here? Mining Town*. Ann Arbor, MI: Cherry Lake Publishing, 2014.

McDowell, Pamela. *Coal Miner*. New York, NY: AV2 Media/ Weigl, 2015.

BIBLIOGRAPHY

Arboriculture Canada. "Back-cuts, Hinges & Control."
     July 2016. https://www.arborcanada.com/blog/back-cuts
     -hinges-control-article-6.

Bolles, Albert S. "Old West Legends: Mining History in the
     United States." Retrieved October 30, 2017. https://www
     .legendsofamerica.com/we-mininghistory.html.

Bureau of Labor Statistics. "Occupational Outlook
     Handbook." Retrieved November 20, 2017.
     https://www.bls.gov/ooh.

Catalyst.org. "Catalyst.org. Women in Male-Dominated
     Industries and Occupations." May 30, 2017.
     http://www.catalyst.org/knowledge/women-male
     -dominated-industries-and-occupations.

Department of Forest Services. "U.S. Forest Resource Facts and
     Historical Trends." United States Department of Agriculture,
     August 2014. https://www.fia.fs.fed.us/library/brochures
     /docs/2012/ForestFacts_1952-2012_English.pdf.

Hammond, Terry, ed. *Yarding and Loading Handbook*.
     Oregon Occupational Safety and Health Standards, 1994.
     https://digital.osl.state.or.us/islandora/object
     /osl%3A3616/datastream/OBJ/view.

History.com. "Ax Men: History of Logging." November 2017.
     http://www.history.co.uk/shows/ax-men/articles/history
     -of-logging.

Lyatsky, Henry. "Magnetic and Gravity Methods in Mineral
     Exploration: The Value of Well-Rounded Geophysical Skills."
     Recorder, Vol. 35, No. 08, Oct. 2010. https://csegrecorder
     .com/articles/view/magnetic-and-gravity-methods-in-mineral
     -exploration.

Midwest Industrial Supply, Inc. "Top 10 Minerals Mined in the U.S." July 21, 2016. http://blog.midwestind.com /top-10-minerals-mined-in-the-u.

Occupational Safety & Health Administration. "Felling Trees: Making the Cuts." Retrieved November 20, 2017. https://www.osha.gov/SLTC/etools/logging/manual /felling/cuts.html.

Pacific Forest Foundation. "Heavy Equipment Operation." Retrieved November 20, 2017. https://www.pacificforestfoundation.org/heavy -equipment-operation.

Pacific Forest Foundation. "Logging Crew." https://www .pacificforestfoundation.org/logging-crew.

Phifer, Maurie, and Hem, Priyadarshi. "TechnoMine: Blasting." *InfoMine*, March 2012. http://technology. infomine.com/reviews/Blasting/welcome.asp?view=full.

Recruiter.com. "Rock Splitters, Quarry." https://www .recruiter.com/careers/rock-splitters-quarry.

StateUniversity.com. "Mining Technician Job Description." Retrieved November 20, 2017. http://careers.stateuniversity .com/pages/37/Mining-Technician.html.

Virginia Department of Forestry. "Select Cutting: Method of Harvesting Trees." Retrieved November 15, 2017. http://www.dof.virginia.gov/manage/harvest/select -cutting.htm.

Wood Splitters Direct. "The Amazing History of Logging in the United States." Retrieved November 15, 2017. https://www.woodsplitterdirect.com/the-amazing -history-of-logging-in-the-united-states.

INDEX

ABOUT THE AUTHOR

A writer and editor living in upstate New York, Jeanne Nagle has written books on a variety of subjects, including careers and employment. Among her many titles are *Careers in Coaching*, *Careers in Computer Technology*, *Careers in Internet Advertising and Marketin*g, *Careers in Television*, and *Jump-Starting a Career in Health Information, Communication & Record Keeping*.

PHOTO CREDITS

Cover, p. 3 Thomas Soellner/Shutterstock.com; p. 6–7 Tyler Stableford/Stone/Getty Images; pp. 11, 34, 40, 59 Bloomberg /Getty Images; p. 12 bondgrunge/iStock/Thinkstock; pp. 15, 26, 42 Colorado School of Mines; p. 20 Graeme Williams /Gallo Images/Getty Images; p. 23 Monty Rakusen/Cultura /Getty Images; p. 30 Phovoir/Shutterstock.com; p. 36 Thomas Samson/AFP/Getty Images; p. 44 Worachat Tokaew /Shutterstock.com; pp. 46, 64 Mark Agnor/Shutterstock.com; p. 47 Bob Pool/Photographer's Choice/Getty Images; p. 50 Design Pics/David Ponton/Getty Images; p. 52 Noah Clayton /Getty Images; p. 55 Tracy Barbutes/Perspectives/Getty Images; p. 57 Farm Images/Universal Images Group/Getty Images; p. 62 MimaCZ/Thinkstock.com; p. 66 TFoxFoto /Shutterstock.com; interior pages background (coal) Patty Chan/Shutterstock.com.

Design: Nelson Sá; Layout: Nicole Russo-Duca; Editor: Philip Wolny; Photo Researcher: Ellina Litmanovich